W9-AYD-466

The Turning of the Year

BILL MARTIN JR

ILLUSTRATED BY GREG SHED

VOYAGER BOOKS

HARCOURT, INC.

Orlando Austin New York San Diego Toronto London

Text copyright © 1970 by Harcourt, Inc., and renewed 1998 by Bill Martin Jr
Illustrations copyright © 1998 by Greg Shed

All rights reserved. No part of this publication may be reproduced or transmitted in any form or by any means, electronic or mechanical, including photocopy, recording, or any information storage and retrieval system, without permission in writing from the publisher.

For information about permission to reproduce selections from this book, write to trade.permissions@hmhco.com or to Permissions, Houghton Mifflin Harcourt Publishing Company, 3 Park Avenue, 19th Floor, New York, New York 10016.

www.hmhco.com

First Voyager Books edition 2007

Voyager Books is a trademark of Harcourt, Inc., registered in the United States of America and/or other jurisdictions.

The Library of Congress has cataloged the hardcover edition as follows:
Martin, Bill, 1916–
The turning of the year/Bill Martin, Jr.; [illustrated by] Greg Shed.
p. cm.
Summary: Describes the characteristics of each month in rhyming text and illustrations.
[1. Months—Fiction. 2. Stories in rhyme.] I. Shed, Greg, ill. II. Title.
PZ7.M3643Tu 1998
[E]—dc21 96-53078
ISBN 978-0-15-201085-0
ISBN 978-0-15-204555-5 pb

PHX 4500830849

The illustrations in this book were done in designer gouache on canvas.
The display type was set in Goudy Village Italic.
The text type was set in Kennerley.
Color separations were made by United Graphic Pte. Ltd., Singapore.
Manufactured in USA
Production supervised by Christine Witnik
Designed by Kaelin Chappell

For Danielle and Rudy
—B. M.

For Chanel and Trent
—G. S.

In January, out I go
to welcome winter's icy blow.

In February, bound with snow,
I sled the hillside, top to toe.

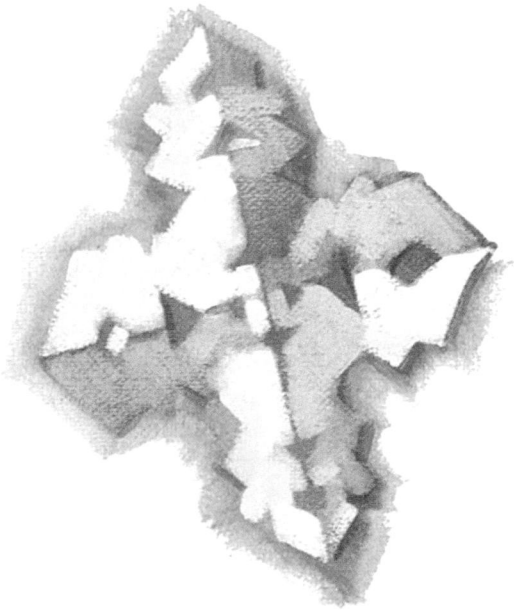

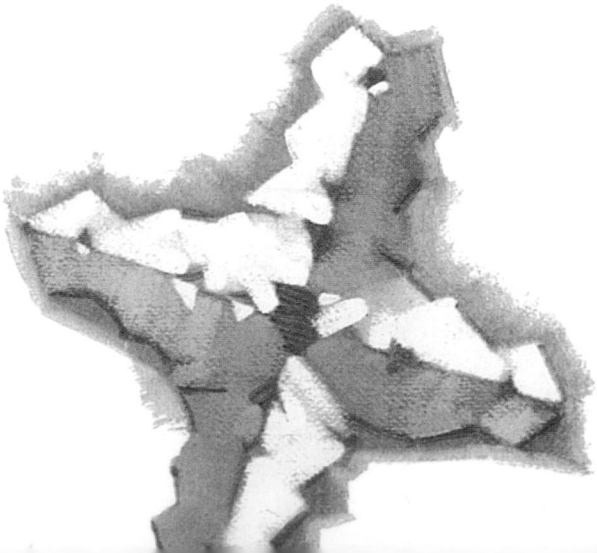

In March,
the warming noontime sun
spells the end
to winter's run.

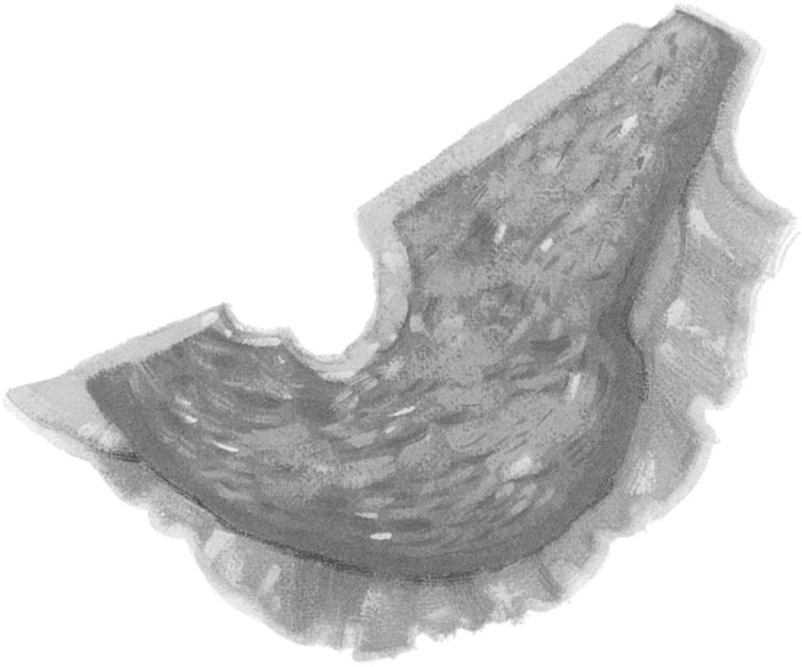

In April, springtime sets me free
to splash through puddles recklessly.

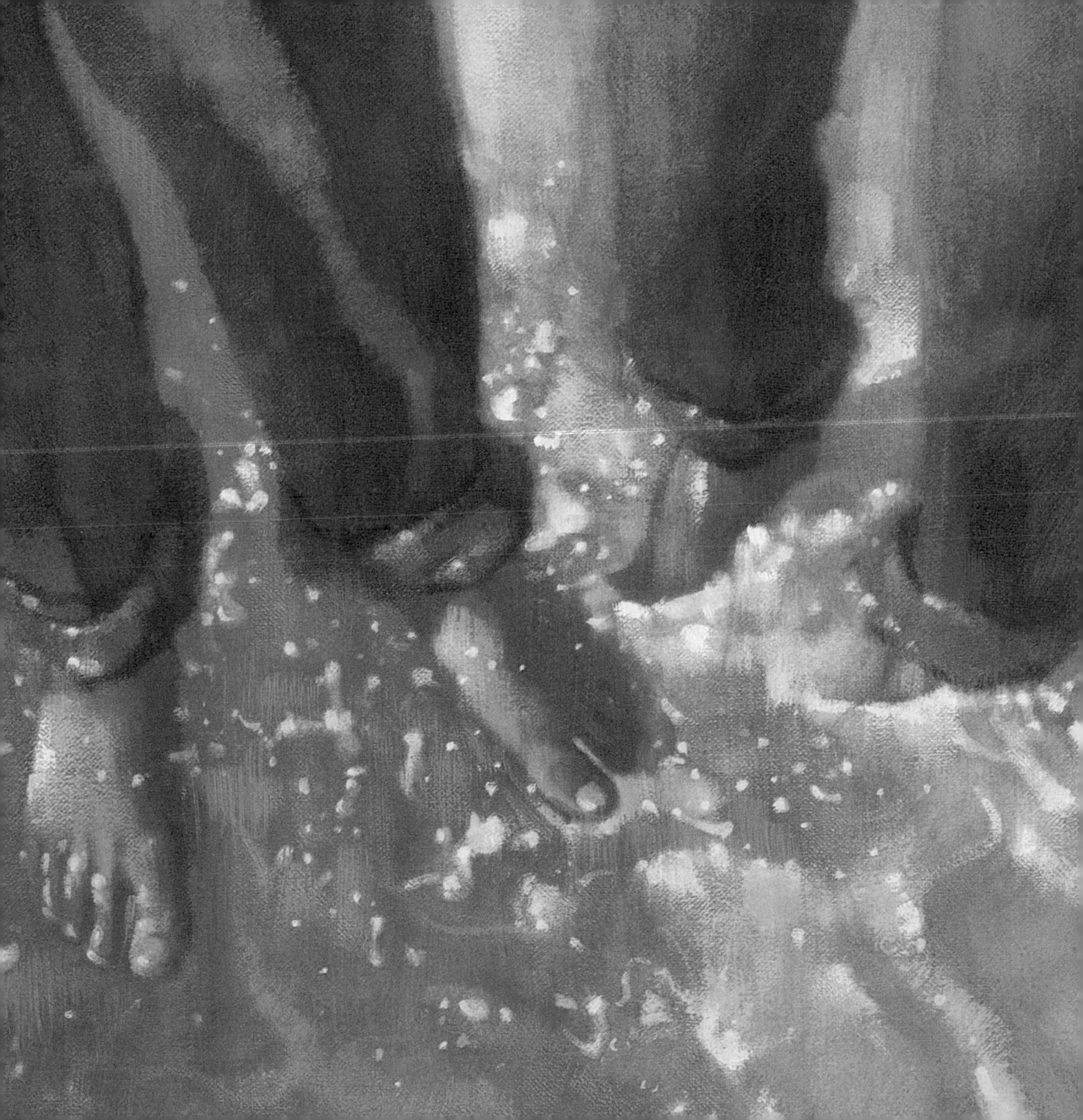

In May, strong branches dare me be
a squirrel in the apple tree.

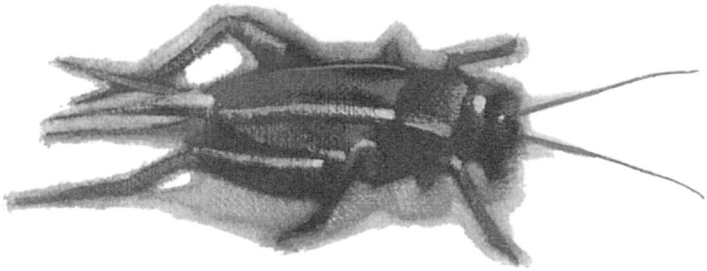

In June,
the warm earth fashions green
and insects sing
good-bye to spring.

In July, summer calls me come
to taste the ripening wild plum.

In August, on hot days I run
through harvest fields that praise the sun.

COUNTY FAIR

In September,
summer calls its ending
with blue haze
and chrysanthemums blending.

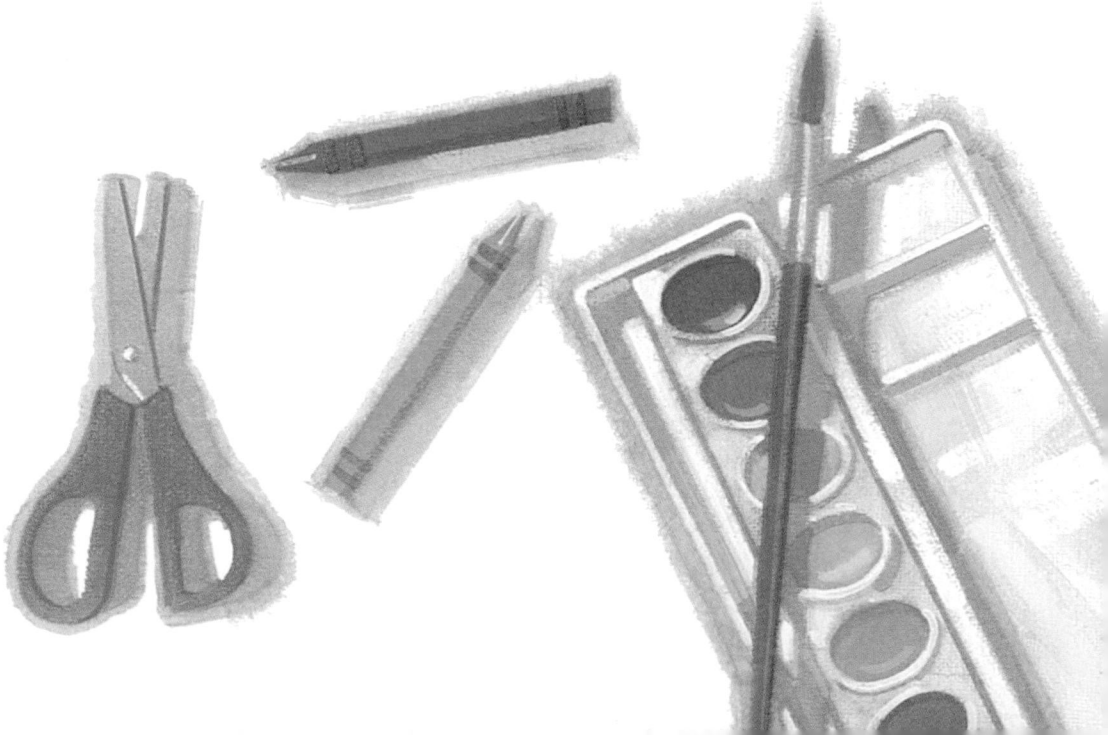

In October, autumn calls me out
to see the maples' raucous shout.

In November, cool days lure me out
to gather pumpkins strewn about.

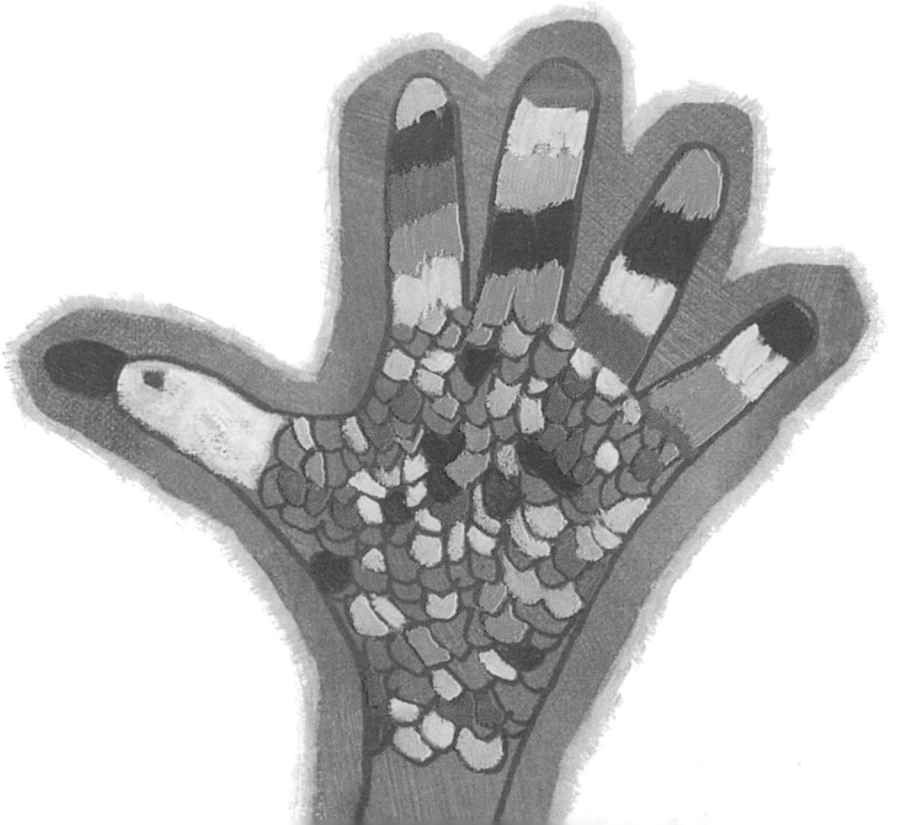

In December,
autumn calls its warning,
"Get ready
for a winter morning!"

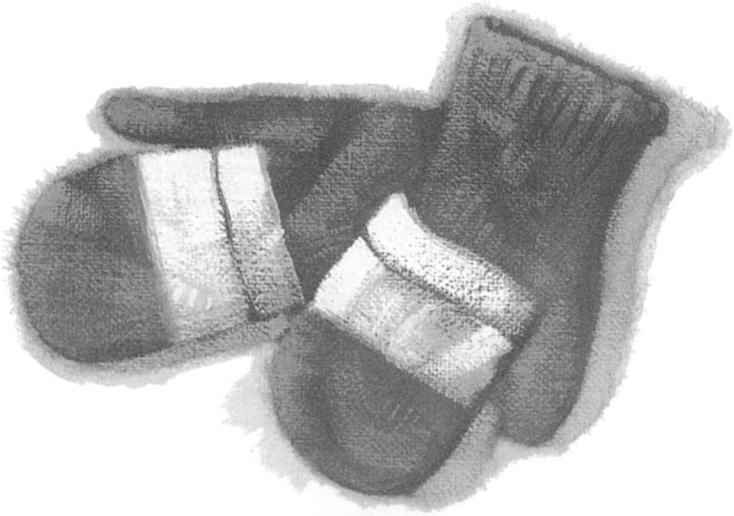